CANDY

The Turkey Who Missed Christmas

GRANDMA GENY HEYWOOD

AuthorHouse™
1663 Liberty Drive
Bloomington, IN 47403
www.authorhouse.com
Phone: 833-262-8899

Because of the dynamic nature of the Internet, any web addresses or links contained in this book may have changed since publication and may no longer be valid. The views expressed in this work are solely those of the author and do not necessarily reflect the views of the publisher, and the publisher hereby disclaims any responsibility for them.

Any people depicted in stock imagery provided by Getty Images are models, and such images are being used for illustrative purposes only.
Certain stock imagery © Getty Images.

This book is printed on acid-free paper.

ISBN: 978-1-4567-1044-6 (sc)
ISBN: 978-1-4685-8858-3 (e)

Library of Congress Control Number: 2010918715

Print information available on the last page.

Published by AuthorHouse

Rev. Date: 11/16/2021

authorHOUSE®

PLEASE CHILDREN,

Pick up a good book and

READ,READ,READ

Your video games may disappoint you, your friends might move away, your computer could fail, but a good book will never let you down, it will always be ready for you to READ,READ,READ

It is very early Christmas Eve at the Heywoodsville homestead; it is also a very cold morning. The old farmer and his wife are busy loading their truck. They are going to sell their goods at the city market to folks eager to purchase organic produce. Together, the old couple lifts onto the platform of the vehicle, big bags of potatoes, a few bushels of turnips and a variety of other vegetables. Then a few Christmas trees are securely tied in two bundles on each side of the load. Between the tree bundles, the farmers secure a wooden crate inside which is a big fat turkey. As they raise the crate onto the load, they try to appear cheerful while exchanging funny jokes but deep inside they feel very sad.

CANDY, the turkey seated in the wooden crate, has been their pet for the last few months. They named her CANDY because of her sweet disposition. They took her in their heart as a new born bird when they noticed her trotting happily and scratching the ground amongst a small regiment of chicks, tiny yellow balls of fluff half her size.

If you are wondering how this newcomer had found herself a boarder at the Heywoodsville farm, here is the story:

CANDY's birth mother, a young eager exploring and wandering wild turkey hen, had strayed away from her flock (actually it's called a "rafter" but the word "flock" is often used), attracted by the smell coming from a pile of manure on the side of the nearby chicken coop. Thus she had wandered away from the bush land onto the farm territory. After surveying the compost offerings, she had felt a sudden urge to sit down. Undisturbed, she had laid, a one and only egg among other smaller ones in the bottom nest of that said hen house. Separated this way from her family by her mistaken curiosity, but somewhat attracted by the comfort of this domestic fowl abode, she had fallen asleep and found herself locked in for the night. Feeling for the first time in her life securely protected against the night dangers of the wild life in the open, she had made the best of this strange situation and had just lain herself there in total physical well-being.

In the morning, having no choice but to leave her egg on the straw with the others, she had left without asking questions as soon as the door of the coop had been unlocked. Zooming by the feet of the old farmer who sleepily had come to open the door, the wild turkey hen birth mother knew very well that she was never to return. However, she rightfully guessed that her progeniture would easily be adopted by some of the old maids chickens eager to care for her egg because of their maternal instinct.

Since domestic fowls are always very obliging and ready to sit patiently on anything with a spheroid shape, eventually, a baby wild turkey had seen the light among the mixed collection of chicks that made the Bantams-Leghorns congregation. The mother hens being all gallinaceans and therefore related to the wild turkey family had sat for their regular shifts during 21 days, apparently ignorant of the exact incubation time. A little surprised at the delay in the hatching of this one larger specimen, the hens had taken turn sitting on that egg for an entire extra week. And this is how it came to pass that last spring a wild turkey baby girl was born at the Heywoodsville farm and was named CANDY.

So now on this very Christmas Eve early morn, Candy, now about 8 months old, sits happily in her crate, proud to have been selected to accompany her surrogate human parents to the city market. She thinks it is a great honor to be chosen for such an expedition but the other animals of the farm that are left in the barn do not have the heart to tell her that being chosen Christmas Turkey is not such a good thing after all.

At last they drive away and after what appears to our CANDY to have been a very long and shaky journey, they arrive in sight of the city.

At a sharp turn from the country road onto the main highway, a tire of the old truck hits a rock, the crate tumbles off the load and comes crashing down onto the pavement. CANDY finds herself free, unhurt, but rather annoyed at being left behind. The old farmers do not even notice the incident and drive on. At first CANDY tries to run after them but to no avail. Disappointed at having missed the big city market expedition, she decides that she must start walking home. What else is there to do?

She is threatened by big dogs straining on their chains at almost every farm house that she walks by. Their barking worries CANDY and she is glad to see them tied up. Only her huge gait saves her from the small yapping dogs on the loose.

While crossing a field, CANDY meets a fox who puts on a good show of mutual regards and pretends to want her as a friend. Oh! He is ever so polite, so sweet towards our young turkey. The excited fox, fueling the conversation, flatters her to no end while stroking his whiskers: "How big and beautiful you are" says the fox…"you look like such an educated bird, such colorful feathers, and look at those eyes, my family would be so honored to make your acquaintance, why don't you come and have dinner with us in our den?"

CANDY has often heard the animals back at the farm speak of the fox, this character that sneaks in unlocked chicken coops at night and kidnaps laying hens and capons alike. At first our young turkey feels flattered by all that attention but then suddenly she realizes that it is a trap. She replies:" No thank you Mr. Fox, I would rather keep on going, I would not want to miss Christmas day at the Heywoodsville farm with all my friends".

But the fox knows a good thing when he sees one and he insists. When with his teeth he decides to grab CANDY by her wing, our turkey lets the biggest gobble-gobble sound you ever heard and lands a strong knock of her powerful beak on the fox's head.

This action frightens the fox that momentarily lets go of the wing. In an instant, CANDY in all her fattened weight is on top of the bushy tail canine, holding him flat to the ground while pecking at his nose with fury.

This does it; the fox decides that this meal is causing way too much trouble, finally, freeing himself, bloody nose and all, he runs away.

Shaken up, our CANDY hurries through the underbrush of the forest. After having gone for what appears a very long distance running and jumping at every noise, she meets with a man who corners her behind a cedar hedge and grabs her by the neck. He drops her in a gunny sac and starts singing...

I was looking for a chicken,

I was looking for a hen,

But what have I just found?

A turkey, nice and round.

Now I am so merry

I'll eat her with chutney,

I'll even add mushrooms,

Chestnuts and cranberry...

Poor CANDY! Now she is really in trouble. Why should the man want to eat her she thinks? Our bird has but one thought in mind: to escape. She must think of something to do and do it fast.

With a big thrust of her powerful beak, she jabs at whatever part of the man she can get at, through the gunny sack, and by pure chance lands him a big whack on the back of the neck.

Surprised and hurt, the fellow lets go of his grip on the sac and it falls to the ground. CANDY does not waste any time. She rushes out of the sac, runs away as fast as her legs can carry her under the ferns and barberry bushes. She must at all cost get away from that kidnapper. At first the man, picking up the empty sac, runs and tries to catch up with CANDY but he soon has to give up the chase, having lost track of his prey.

Candy is feeling very sad. Night is coming and she is not at all sure of the way home. Having been on the road the whole day, she is very tired. While passing near a country church, she hears sounds of music and carol singing within. "Oh Dear me" she says "Why is everybody so happy, so merry? Here I am, all alone and lost in the woods…and of all nights, on Christmas Eve! How shall I ever make it home in time for the Christmas celebration? I heard the animals of the farm speak of nothing else for the last few weeks".

So she hurries on. An owl, who has just overheard her lament, lands next to her on the ground and starts talking to CANDY: "Whoo, whoo, whoo are you? And why are you rushing home, don't you know that humans eat turkeys at Christmas?"

Now CANDY really worries, for a while there, she thought that maybe she had misunderstood the intentions of the man who threw her in the gunny sac. Surely her very own human folk at Heywoodsville farm would not eat her. The owl suggests that if CANDY was being taken to market it must have been that they did not have the heart to use her as the center piece of the Christmas feast on their own dining room table. It is a well known fact he says that humans let others do what they do not want to do themselves. "The dirty work...you know; Sad, but true" the owl said.

"Well, anyhooo" concludes the owl, "let them eat cake, Christmas cake...merry Christmas to them, and you make sure you save yourself young turkey"... then he flies away.

"What am I to do?" says CANDY to herself "I am tired, I am cold, I am hungry, I am thirsty, and I feel very unhappy".

Searching on the ground, she picks at some seeds and thinks it is nothing to compare to the big bowl of steaming mush she used to get three times a day at her farm. Looking for some water to drink, she stumbles and slides down in a ditch only to crash through the ice.

-"I wanted water, but surely not under those circumstances. Now I am wet and very very cold".

To make matters worse, snow starts falling, poor conditions for a wet turkey travelling through the country.

Having twisted her leg in the fall, CANDY limps to a hollow log that she sees lying on the mossy ground. As she pushes her body into the open end of the log, she frightens a family of rabbits who has already settled down for the night.

-"Don't be afraid little friends" says CANDY "I will not bother you, all I really need is a good night's rest and first thing in the morning, I shall leave".

Reassured, and anxious to hear the turkey's story, the rabbits relax and listen attentively to the account of the past day as told by our CANDY. The rabbits are most sympathetic and offer her many words of comfort.

-"What is your plan" finally asks father rabbit whose name by the way is Jack.

-"I guess I have no choice but to return home" says CANDY, "I could never live in the bush the way you rabbits do. And, I am not really a wild turkey able to find my own food either because I was raised on a farm. I am only what you call a domestic bird used to being fed by humans. Mind you, they do feed us well, hot corn mush at every meal, at least three times a day, sometimes four".

The rabbits are astonished at this news, "you are lucky" says mother rabbit "we always have to find our own food while avoiding snares and large attackers". CANDY thinks for a moment then says: "I start to wonder if I really am that lucky".

They all fall asleep but CANDY spends a restless night. Ghosts of Christmas turkeys appear to her in dreams telling her that they were served as food, served on big platters as meals for humans.

When finally she wakes up from her nightmares, she bids goodbye to the rabbits, thanks them for their hospitality then gets on the road again having declined to accompany them on their breakfast search. She will find food for strength as she goes along her way she says. Time is of the essence if she wants to get to the farm before night comes again leaving Christmas day and the celebrations behind.

She is now following a river bank through the thick bush and has no way of knowing that it is actually the river that crosses her farm at the bottom of the acreage. She sits down to relax and meditate for a while and tries to listen for whatever sound or whatever smell might come her way to give her some indication of where she is. The natural GPS of her brain tells her that yes she is going in the right direction if only she can stay out of human sight. So she keeps on walking.

At this point, CANDY walks by a huge earthwork, a build up of steaming earth and branches that reminds her of a giant bowl of corn mush. Curious to know what it is, she ventures closer but is met by a furious beaver repairing his lodge. In her eagerness CANDY has ventured on a frozen beaver pond.

..."get away from my home you big wobbly feathery thing, can't you see that I am busy repairing my roof?" says the beaver...

"I am going I am going right now" says CANDY and she hurries away.

In the distance she hears cars driving on a country road and at times human voices exchanging friendly greetings and shouting to one another:" Merry Christmas, Merry Christmas".

She now wonders about her humans 'reaction when the day before, they arrived at the city market and found their turkey crate missing from the back of the truck. Of course they must have safely returned home with the empty truck by now. She imagines them serving that delicious corn mush to all the animals in the barn.

CANDY suddenly reaches a clearing in the bush and sees children playing hockey on a frozen creek.

She stops in her tracks right there. She is afraid to have been seen, but the children do not even notice CANDY. They are far more interested in playing with their brand new hockey equipment: skates, helmets and sticks that surprised them under their decorated tree when they woke up this Christmas morning.

Our CANDY backs up slowly, not making a sound and walks far away from the danger spot. She is not about to take more chances than absolutely necessary.

And so Christmas day goes by, a little less traumatic than the day before, on Christmas Eve when everybody was tormenting her and trying to catch her for their dinner.

On and on our poor exhausted CANDY walks. She keeps in the underbrush as much as possibly feasible.

Then suddenly in the late afternoon she meets with a slow walking porcupine who introduces himself as Spikes.

He tells her that he is afraid of nobody. Why should he be? When your entire body is covered with a coat made from sharp darning needles, who do you think, in their right mind would be silly enough to try picking you up or stroking your back?

-"Where are you going big turkey?" asks Spikes "it is late and it will be dark soon, Christmas is almost over, why are you in the woods at this hour? How can I help you?"

Sensing that Spikes is a true friendly creature, CANDY tells him of her misadventures and explains to the porcupine that all she needs now is to find her farm.

-"I know that it should not be very far, after all I have been on the road for two days".

Obligingly, Spikes climbs up a tall pine tree and describes to CANDY what he sees in the distance:

-"I see...a big barn with a red door".

-"Yes, yes, Spikes, what else do you see?"

-"I see a cute little farm house with lots of windows".

-"Yes, yes, Spikes" says our turkey getting all excited, "What else, Spikes, what else can you see?"

-"There is an old school bus in the yard and a big letter H over the entrance of the driveway".

-"That's it Spikes, that's it, that's my farm, that's my home, how far is it, please, can you tell me?"

While climbing down from the tree like an experienced telephone repair person coming down a pole, Spikes gives proper directions to CANDY, then pushes her gently away with the tip of his finger nails... "Keep on going my friend, keep on going fast, it is not too far. You would not want to spend another night outside, would you...hurry!"

CANDY thanks the porcupine for his help and finds the strength to walk faster...

It is pitch black outside when CANDY finally reaches her barn. The door is ajar; she slides inside, and, in absolute exhaustion collapses on the clean fresh bed of hay where her friends are just now settling themselves down for the night.

The Jersey cow, the pig, the chickens, the horse, the sheep and all the other animals have already had their Christmas supper. However CANDY notices that they have left in their trough a big portion of corn mush. She assumes rightfully that it is for her...right here, next to her normal sleeping spot. Seeing CANDY back in their midst, all the animals shout for joy and give her their friendly greetings in their many different languages...yes they all understand each other.

Meanwhile CANDY gorges herself happily, celebrating a late Christmas, at last, with her farm friends, her family.

Suddenly the cat and the dog come rushing into the barn, followed by the two old farmers. The old couple wondered what all that commotion was about. At first, CANDY is not sure what is going to happen to her, after all, her humans were ready to sell her at the city market only the day before. What are they going to do to her now?

The old man scratches his head, he is amazed at seeing CANDY back home, he is wondering...

-"Well CANDY" he says "I don't know what happened to you; I bet you have many stories to tell. It is very late, you have missed Christmas day almost entirely but we are sure glad to see you back home where you belong. You will have nothing to worry about from now on. Just enjoy your meal; it is obvious that your animal friends knew that you would come back. I can tell that they have more sense than humans give them credit for".

As the old couple walks away, CANDY hears the wife say:

-"We will make sure that from now on she misses all the Christmases" then she adds: "...and all the Thanksgivings too".

At the top of her lungs, CANDY suddenly explodes in a big shout for joy:

" gobble-gobble-gobble, Am I glad I missed Christmas!"

....THE END..

Printed in the United States
by Baker & Taylor Publisher Services

Printed in the United States
by Baker & Taylor Publisher Services